Book #6

THE SQUIRRELS GO NUTS

Buck Wilder

Other Buck Wilder Books

Buck Wilder's Adventures
#1 Who Stole the Animal Poop?
#2 The Work Bees Go on Strike
#3 The Ants Dig to China
#4 The Owls Don't Give a Hoot
#5 The Salmon Stop Running

Buck Wilder's Animal Wisdom
Buck Wilder's Small Fry Fishing Guide
Buck Wilder's Small Twig Hiking and Camping Guide
Buck Wilder's Little Skipper Boating Guide

...and more to come...

Buck Wilder's Animal Adventures #6: The Squirrels Go Nuts
Written by Timothy R. Smith

First Edition
Library of Congress Cataloging-in-Publication Data

Smith, Timothy R.

Buck Wilder's Adventures #6
The Squirrels Go Nuts

Summary: Buck Wilder and his forest friends try to figure out why the
squirrels have gone missing from the forest.

ISBN: 978-0-9825475-0-2

Fiction
10 9 8 7 6 5 4 3 2

Buck Wilder Adventures
4160 M-72 East
Williamsburg, MI 49690

www.buckwilder.com

Buck Wilder ™

"Every animal has a purpose."
B.W.

THE SQUIRRELS
GO NUTS!

CHAPTERS

Meet Buck Wilder and his family of friends   10

1. IT ALL STARTED LIKE THIS   18
2. THE SQUIRRELS HAVE GONE NUTS 27
3. BE CAREFUL   31
4. GRANDPA GRADY GRAY
     SQUIRREL   40
5. FREE FOOD   52
6. RASCAL TELLS ALL   59
7. IT WAS NOT THE NATURAL WAY 67
8. THE BEST THING WE COULD DO 73
9. PLEASE DON'T FEED THE
     ANIMALS   78
10. BACK TO THE NORMAL WAY   83

     Secret message decoding page   87
     If you need help page   88

INTRODUCTION

To meet Buck Wilder you have to walk into the woods, way back into the woods, where he lives. You will find him in a big tree house built among some huge trees. The tree house looks kind of like this:

In the tree house you will find Buck Wilder, usually visiting with some of his animal friends, or cooking a meal that gives you warm dreams, or tinkering with his fishing equipment getting ready to go fishing. He is a very honest, dependable, and friendly man and you would like him.

He looks kind of like this:

Buck Wilder's best friend and loyal companion is a very smart yet mischievous little raccoon. His name is Rascal Raccoon and he is very loyal to Buck Wilder. Rascal knows all the animals in the woods and everyone likes and respects him. He looks kind of like this:

The animals in the woods, who are all friends of Buck Wilder, often come to visit Buck's tree house to tell stories, eat one of Buck's home cooked meals, or to ask Buck for his help in solving some problem or dilemma that is happening among the animals or in the woods. Most often Buck can help. Some of Buck's friends look like this:

Turn the page and read about one of the problems that Buck's animal friends brought to him for his help. It was the time the squirrels went nuts and what Buck did to help solve the problem. Have fun reading!

CHAPTER 1

IT ALL STARTED LIKE THIS

It was a great day to be alive. Buck had gotten up early in the morning, had a big steaming cup of coffee with his breakfast, finished his morning chores and was getting ready to do a little afternoon fishing. Buck just loves to go fishing and knows that anytime is a great time to go fishing. Rascal had fed the pet fish in the aquarium, watered the plants, had completed his morning chores and was looking forward to joining Buck on his afternoon fishing trip. The sun was shining, there was a slight breeze, the leaves were chuckling back and forth, and it looked like a nice and easy day in the life of Buck and Rascal.

Then the visitor's bell began to ring. Anytime Buck Wilder had visitors, they had to pull the string on the visitor's bell which rang inside of Buck's tree house. Rascal Raccoon would then holler down to see who had come to visit, lower the ladder to the tree house, and allow the visitor to come see Buck. Animals came to visit Buck all the time, not just when there was a problem or a dilemma in the woods, but sometimes just to visit, tell stories, or

have something to eat with Buck. Buck was a great cook and liked to share his food with his animal friends, and he had plenty of them.

This day had not brought one visitor, but three. Downstairs pulling the bell cord was Clyde Swan, Jackie Pheasant, and Ollie Opossum. "Come on up," hollered Rascal from up in the tree house. "Here comes the ladder," he

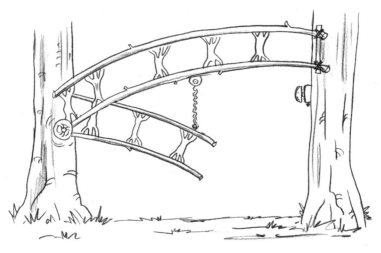

added as he slowly lowered it.

Clyde Swan, Jackie Pheasant, and Ollie Opossum came up the steps and through the hallway, right into Buck's kitchen. Without hesitation each jumped up on a stool by the kitchen counter and in almost perfect unison, said, "Did we make it in time for lunch, Buck? We are

a little hungry and you always have the best food in the forest."

"Thanks for the flattery," responded Buck. "I think a little afternoon lunch snack would be just fine. I haven't seen the three of you in a month of Sundays, so having you join me at the table would be my honor. Remember though, I cook 'people food' which is a lot different than your wild animal food, so don't eat too much because it may upset your stomachs."

"We know, Buck," replied all three, "but a little of your good cooking goes a long way with us."

"Okay," said Buck. "How about a few little whole grain pancakes with some fresh wild fruit on top? Clyde, I could put a few blueberries on yours. Jackie, you could get some raspberries, and Ollie, how about some crushed nuts in yours?"

"Yummy," replied all three. "Yes, please."

"Okay," said Buck. "While I am getting things ready, tell me what is going on. Any new stories in the woods, friends? Pull your chairs up close, sit up straight, hats off at the table, and use your best manners." Buck was always big on manners, especially table manners, and would often remind his animal friends that you show respect through manners and that you should always show your best.

Ollie Opossum spoke up first while pulling his chair closer to the counter. "Wow, it will be great to take off this hard hat. My ears get all crinkled inside and sometimes it gets a little hot in here."

"Why the hard hats?" asked Buck as he mixed a bowl of pancake batter.

"I think I can speak for the three

Wow, what whacked you?

of us," said Ollie Opossum as he looked at the other two.

"Sure, we all have the same problem," said Jackie Pheasant.

"What is that?" asked Buck with a little surprised look on his face.

"It is a big problem and we all have it," responded Ollie. "Just take a

look at this," said Ollie as hc pointed to a big ol' knot on the top of his head. "And take a look at those," he said as he pointed to the heads of his companions, each showing big swollen welts on the top of their heads.

"What happened to you guys?" Buck put down his mixing bowl, walked over and took a closer look. "Wow, those are some real knobs on your noggins. What hit you guys on the head?"

CHAPTER 2

THE SQUIRRELS HAVE GONE NUTS

"The squirrels did it," said Ollie Opossum. "They pelted us with nuts and I don't know why. Whack, boom—there are nuts flying all over the place. There is not a safe place in the woods to walk without a nut coming at you. We don't know what is going on, but the squirrels have definitely gone nuts, and there are not enough hard hats to

27

go around. Most of the animals are in hiding, afraid to venture out into the woods because they know they will be whacked by a nut. It is really dangerous out there. The forest floor is covered with nuts and we don't know what to do. Can you help us, Buck? We've got a real problem out there." By this time Rascal had moved in closer to take a look at their swollen heads.

28

"Sure, I would be glad to help, but before I do, let's eat these pancakes. Things always seem to go better with a little food in the stomach." Buck dished out the pancakes and put the wild fruit and nuts on top. Good manners were used by all with a big "Thank you, Buck!" and everyone pitched in on the clean up.

"I guess I can go fishing later," said Buck, looking at his fishing equipment. "Seems like I am needed more in other places. Rascal, again, this sounds like a job for you. We need a little investigative work, a little detective work to find out what is going on and I know of no one better than you for the job." Rascal stood up straight, almost at attention, upon hearing the compliment from Buck.

"Tell me what to do, Buck. I am always glad to help," said Rascal.

"Here is what I think you should do," said Buck. "Simply go with Ollie Opossum, Jackie Pheasant, and Clyde Swan back out into the woods. Take a look around and see what is going on. Ask some questions, check it out, be the great detective that you are and find out what is the matter with the squirrels. Why have they apparently gone nuts?"

CHAPTER 3

BE CAREFUL

So, off went Ollie Opossum, Jackie Pheasant, and Clyde Swan with Rascal in the lead. They went down Buck's hallway, down the ladder, and out into the woods. They didn't move too fast because Ollie Opossum was with them and he was one of the slowest moving animals in the woods. Sometimes he would just stop in his tracks and fall over, playing dead. It was a game he always played and he liked to practice it. The other animals never really understood, but they tolerated his behavior and accepted him as he was—a little different. Animals are like that— very accepting. Clyde Swan wasn't much faster either because of his big webbed feet. He could move across the water like greased lighting, but when it came to walking on land he just poked along. It was hardest on Jackie Pheasant because she was one of the fastest in the woods. Rascal, who prided himself on his speed and always challenged others to a race, would never challenge Jackie Pheasant. He knew that Jackie was not only one of the fastest birds to fly, but he also knew there wasn't anything in the woods faster than a running pheasant.

Then Rascal spoke up. "If you all don't mind, I am just going to move off on my own and do a little investigating. I am going to head directly toward those big acorn and walnut trees and see what is going on."

"Be careful," said Ollie. "Those squirrels have nuts flying everywhere. Here, do you want to borrow my hard hat?"

"No, thanks," replied Rascal. "I'll be just fine…See you all later and thanks for letting Buck know about the problem. It gives me a job to work on and makes me feel kind of important. Bye!" And off they all went in different directions.

It didn't take long before Rascal was right in the middle of it all. Sure enough, the floor of the woods which was usually fairly clean and only covered with a few leaves, pine needles, and an occasional dead branch was now literally covered with nuts. Acorns, walnuts, and a few other local nuts from the big old trees now covered the entire forest floor. There was no place to walk

without stepping on some kind of nut. And what made matters worse was they were coming down like hail from the sky.

Whop! Right on Rascal's forehead, right between the ears. "Oww! That hurt, stop that! Who threw that?" There was no answer, almost a quiet in the trees, but the nuts kept coming down. "I'm going home for a football helmet and

not coming back until I have some nut protection." Rascal quickly turned in his tracks and without hesitation took off for Buck's tree house.

When he got back to Buck's tree house he told Buck about all the nuts on the forest floor, how fast they came flying out of the trees, and then showed him the big pine cone welt on the top of his head.

"Ooo," said Buck, taking a closer look. "That's a good one!" Buck reached into the freezer. "Here is a little bag of frozen blueberries to put on it. It will help the swelling go down."

"Rascal, I think you should take a little rest and maybe tonight before dark, if you are up to it, head back to the acorn forest and do a little more detective work. Stake it out, spend the night, be there in the morning and find out what the squirrels are up to. Then

Can I eat these blueberries?

come back and let me know. The more facts I have the better I can help."

"Okay Buck," said Rascal as he lay down in his typical curled-up sleeping position and took a quick nap. When he awoke his head felt much better. The frozen blueberries had taken the swelling down. He felt like he was ready to go again. He grabbed a football helmet from the sports chest and down the ladder he went.

CHAPTER 4

GRANDPA GRADY GRAY SQUIRREL

It was beginning to get dark in the woods, the quiet time when most of the color leaves and everything turns into more black and white. Luckily for Rascal he was a raccoon and had outstanding night vision and could see as well in the dark as he could in the day. When he reached the acorn forest where the big oak trees lived he climbed a nearby tree looking for a good place to sleep for the night. Rascal loves to climb trees, especially in the dark. He found a big tree hole between two branches, which surprisingly looked like an abandoned squirrel's house, climbed in, snuggled up, and listened closely to the woods. It was quiet, really quiet. So quiet that before long Rascal fell sound asleep, snoring quietly as the night winds blew through the trees. The only things out that night were the bright stars and the owl time keepers of the woods.

In the morning, the woods came alive with the chatter of animals talking, birds calling, insects buzzing, and the color of the day had come back. Rascal was looking and listening from his hole

in the tree. Everything seemed fairly normal in the woods except for the squirrels, or from what he saw, the lack of the squirrels. Something was very wrong. They were gone. He couldn't see a squirrel anywhere. This was very puzzling to Rascal and as he sat there looking and listening for the squirrels he heard old Grandpa Grady Gray Squirrel coming down the limb toward him. Grandpa Grady Gray Squirrel was moving really slow, a little hunched over in age, and walking with the help of a wooden cane in one hand. "Good morning," said Grandpa Grady Gray Squirrel. "I saw you come in last night and climb into the old Swanson Squirrel house. They moved off, you know, took a job somewhere else. I don't know where they went. Heard you sleeping last night. You put out a pretty good snore!"

"Where is everybody?" asked Rascal.

"Huh?" replied Grandpa Grady Gray Squirrel through the few teeth that he had left. He was hard of hearing and most often you had to repeat yourself, and louder each time.

"Where did all the squirrels go?" shouted Rascal in an extra loud voice.

"Oh, they just moved off. Little by little, they have all packed up and moved. Whole families of them. Nothing is the same around here. There is but a handful left, the rest of 'em are just gone."

"Where did they go?" asked Rascal, much louder this time.

"I don't know. The place isn't the same with them not around here. Look at all those nuts. The trees are full of them, the ground is full of them. They're just lying around everywhere."

"Why so many nuts?" asked Rascal, keeping his voice at almost a shout level.

"Most years you get a few nuts off these trees, but every once and a while you get a gangbuster year like this one. There are so many nuts on those trees that every time the wind blows just a little, the sky falls with 'em. You can't even walk on the forest floor without crushing a few nut shells with every step."

"Em," thought Rascal to himself. "That must be why everyone is getting hit on the head with flying nuts. There are more nuts than normal and the squirrels are gone. Makes sense, but what doesn't make sense is why the squirrels have gone, and where did they go?"

"I think its going to be a tough winter," shouted Grandpa Grady Gray Squirrel. "Those nuts are falling early and there are a lot of them. I think it's nature's way of telling us to get ready for a tough one!"

"Interesting," said Rascal.

"Huh?" responded Grandpa Grady.

"I said, that is very interesting," said Rascal almost shouting.

"What is interesting is that Smith family over there. Look at 'em. They are one of the last squirrel families left

in these parts. They are all packed up and they are leaving too."

"I don't know what is going to happen to this place, but right now I don't care. I am going to go back and take a nap. The older I get, seems like the more naps I want to take."

"Have a good one," said Rascal.

"Huh?" again from Grandpa Grady.

"Have a good nap!" shouted Rascal.

"Oh, yeah. Thanks. Bye," and off went Grandpa Grady Gray Squirrel in a slow shuffle.

"I think I will follow that Smith family and see where they are going," thought Rascal. And so he did. Slowly Rascal climbed down the tree, being very careful not to make much noise.

Raccoons are good at that. He got into his detective mode and began to very quietly follow the Smith Squirrel family through the woods. It wasn't very easy following squirrels through the woods because squirrels tend to travel by jumping from tree to tree and running along the branches. Rascal had to follow by hiding behind trees and running to keep up. It was somewhat difficult, but Rascal could do it. They went a long way, traveling most of the morning to the outside edge of the forest and kept going through the fields all the way to the big city. Rascal stayed way back and kept watching. To his surprise the squirrels did not stop at the edge of the big city, as most animals naturally do, but just kept going. Rascal went as far as he thought was safe because he knew raccoons did not belong in the city and it would be dangerous for him. There are a lot of people there and they drive big cars! Rascal climbed the closest and tallest tree he could find and just watched. What he saw was this!

CHAPTER 5

FREE FOOD

The Smith Squirrel family had headed right into the middle of Central Park, a giant park in the city full of walking trails, a fishing pond with ducks on it, benches to sit on, and lots of clean clear cut grass. In the park were people running as if they were being chased, dogs pulling people on leashes, kids trying to skip stones across the pond, and people on the grass having picnics. It looked like a happy place. The one thing that didn't look right and surprised Rascal the most was the number of people who were feeding the animals. There were kids throwing pieces of bread to the ducks. There was a lady on the bench throwing popcorn to the birds and there was the answer to what Rascal had been looking for: people were throwing nuts to the squirrels, all kinds of nuts, and all kinds of squirrels! Brown squirrels, red squirrels, black squirrels—whole families of them, dancing, rolling, and gobbling up as many nuts as they could. The Smith Squirrel family had jumped right in. They dropped their luggage and all of their personal belongings at the edge of the park and ran as fast as they could to the free food, and why not? People were throwing to the squirrels every kind of nut you could think of: cashews, pistachios, almonds, peanuts, and macadamia nuts. The shells had already been taken off; many of the nuts were salted or spiced, so the squirrels were just having a ball. They were going nuts eating all they could. It was

like a dream come true. You could hear the people shout with excitement;

"Look at this one—he is eating from my hand!"

"Watch this little one stand on his hind legs and beg for more!"

"Look how many nuts this one can hold in his pudgy cheeks!

And on, and on.

To Rascal it was a sight that was almost unbelievable. No wonder all the squirrels had left the woods. In the park they didn't have to work, make a living, or be responsible and they could eat as much as they wanted and food they had never had before. He actually saw a few squirrels in the corner of the park throwing up from eating spicy chips, over-salted nuts, and from eating too much food that they weren't used to.

Rascal didn't like what he saw because he knew it wasn't the natural way for animals to live, but he didn't know what to do except to go back to Buck and explain what he had seen. Buck's wisdom would know what to do. Rascal climbed down from his tall tree very quietly and slowly so that no one would see him. He headed back the way he had come and felt better being back to his safe and natural woods where he lived. There was something about the city that was unnatural, not safe, and a place that he didn't belong. Off went Rascal.

CHAPTER 6

RASCAL TELLS ALL

It was late in the afternoon by the time Rascal reached Buck's tree house. He was tired from all his detective work and somewhat out of breath from having run most of the way home. When he reached the tree house he ran straight up the ladder, down the hallway, and screeched to a halt in Buck's kitchen.

"Wow, slow down Rascal," said Buck. "You are running like something is chasing you. Are you okay?"

"I…I….I'm fine," said Rascal in an out of breath response. "It's what I saw. You won't believe it. I found out why the squirrels have gone nuts!"

"Okay Rascal, slow down. I want to hear it all. Here, take a drink of water, catch your breath and tell me what you found out."

Rascal then told him everything—how he had slept out all night in an abandoned squirrel house, meeting Grandpa Grady Gray Squirrel, learning that most of the squirrels had left the woods, and how he followed the entire Smith Squirrel family to the city. Then he told Buck about what he saw in the city park.

"Oh no," responded Buck, looking down in a serious manner. "This is a problem, a big one, because of a lot of reasons. First, I want to compliment you, Rascal, on the great detective work. You did an outstanding job. Thanks! You were so right not to go into the city.

You don't belong there. It is not natural for you to be in the city. You could get hurt there. Sometimes people just don't understand."

"What do you mean?" asked Rascal with a questioning look on his face.

"Let me explain," said Buck. "First, feeding wild animals routinely is not natural. It upsets the natural way of life for animals. Animals do not have common sense as most people have. They just respond in a natural way without thinking. Take the squirrels, for example. They have a number of jobs as members of the woods. Their primary job is to clean up all the nuts that fall from the nut trees. They can eat as many as they want, store a bunch away for the long cold winter, and plant the rest for future growth. That future growth supplies our woods with more trees and more nuts for upcoming years."

"The older squirrels teach the younger ones and on it goes, year after year, in the natural way."

"Em," said Rascal, thinking deeply about it.

Buck continued, "Along with the crows, the squirrels are our natural watch dogs of the woods. They will run up a tree and chatter an alarm across the woods in case a wolf, an intruder, or someone that doesn't belong enters the woods. With the squirrels gone, things fall out of place, just like all the nuts that are lying around on the forest floor. It's just not natural.

"Tomorrow, when I get up, I will put on my hiking boots and take a long walk down the trail through our woods that leads to the city. I need to visit Central Park and talk to the Park Ranger that works there and see if anything can be done. The people that work in that park care a lot about nature and I am sure they can help." Buck needed to say no more for Rascal to curl up on his favorite sleeping rug and fall off into a deep sleep.

He was exhausted from all the detective work he had done and was ready to call it a night. "Good night, Rascal," said Buck as he headed toward his bedroom. "I think I'll read for awhile. See you in the morning." The only reply that came from Rascal was a deep long snore.

CHAPTER 7

IT WAS NOT THE NATURAL WAY

As planned, the next morning had Buck and Rascal walking through the woods, heading down the trail that led to the city. When they reached the edge of the woods Buck turned to Rascal and said, "I think it is best if you stay right here. It is a lot safer for you. The city is no place for a raccoon. You are not like a dog or a pet and you belong in the woods."

"I couldn't agree with you more," replied Rascal. "I'll just hang out in one of those trees and keep an eye out for your return."

"Thanks," said Buck and off he walked toward the city. At times Buck liked to visit the city because of all the modern conveniences it had, pick up extra supplies he couldn't get in the woods, or to get a few new books from the city library. Most times it was a fun trip but he sure didn't like all those cars, all those paved streets, and how people tended to live so close to each other, but that is the way cities were and he accepted it.

It didn't take long for him to reach Central Park and see for himself what was happening. Rascal was exactly right. Seagulls were plucking potato chips out of the air, the ducks and geese were quacking and honking for pieces of bread, and the squirrels were almost eating out of people's hands. Nothing was right. It was not the natural way. "I better go see the Park Ranger," said Buck to himself. "He will know what to do."

Buck found the Park Office, introduced himself, and explained why he was there. "Just one moment, Sir," said a very nice lady that was working behind the reception desk. "I'll get Mr. Myka. He is our head Park Ranger and

I am sure he will be glad to talk with you." As she opened an office door she said, "Excuse me, Mr. Myka, but there is a Mr. Buck Wilder here to see you and he says—"

Before she could finish her sentence Mr. Myka blurted out, "Buck Wilder—here to visit me? No way!" He jumped from his chair and almost ran from the office. "Buck, wow, it is good to see you. Been a long time since I've seen your smiling face."

Buck extended his big right hand with a smile, shook hands with the head Park Ranger and said, "Leon, it is good to see you too. The last time we went fishing together you had just joined the park as a service ranger. Now you are the big kahuna running the whole thing. Life must be treating you pretty good!"

"It sure is, Buck," answered Ranger Leon, still smiling. "I am curious to know why you have come to visit me. But more importantly, I would like to know if you are catching any fish?"

"I sure am," answered Buck. "But I'll catch more if you join me. I would like to have you come along sometime."

"Thanks," said Ranger Leon. "But we have been very short handed around here lately and I have been putting in a lot of extra work hours. When things free up I will be out there. Count on it." Ranger Leon put a friendly hand on Buck's shoulder and said, "So, what's up, Buck? How can I help you?"

CHAPTER 8

THE BEST THING WE COULD DO

Buck's face turned to a more serious look as he said, "Leon, I think we have a real problem here in the park. People are feeding the wild animals and, as you know, that is just not right. You know as well as I do that if you feed the bird's everyday they will get real use to coming to your house and eating out of your bird feeder and it becomes their source of food. If for some reason you have to leave your house for some period of time, go on a long vacation, or for whatever reason, those birds come to an empty bird feeder and they don't know what to do, especially the young ones. They don't know where to find seed naturally in the woods. They get hungry and a bunch of them will die. It goes the same with any animal. It causes more harm than the pleasure we get from it."

"You are absolutely right," responded Ranger Leon. "We see that going on all the time, and another thing; most people throw the wrong kind of food to the animals. Wild animals are not supposed to eat greasy potato chips, salted pretzels, and buttered popcorn. That's not natural food for them and causes all kinds of problems with their stomachs. We find sick animals all the time. They start to get fat, lazy, forgetting how to find their own food and before long we will see them going

through the trash barrels looking for easy eats. They will even come up and eat out of people's hands and that is really dangerous."

"Sure is," said Buck, nodding his head in agreement. "Is there anything we can do to let people know that it is not right to feed wild animals?"

"There sure is," responded Ranger Leon. "We have been short staffed in this park for some time now and like I said, I've been putting in extra hours cutting grass, dumping trash barrels, changing lights, and never quite seem to get caught up. I think the best thing we could do," continued Ranger Leon, "is to let people know that it is not right to fool with Mother Nature and put up a bunch of signs that simply say PLEASE DON'T FEED THE ANIMALS."

"I would be glad to help you," responded Buck. "Let's put them everywhere—by the lake, next to the benches, and along the park trails. I am sure that will help and maybe once in a while you could have a nature program here at the park office explaining the hazards of feeding wild life."

"Good idea," said Ranger Leon. "Thanks, and I sure could use your help."

CHAPTER 9

PLEASE DON'T FEED THE ANIMALS

For the rest of that day Buck helped Ranger Leon make up a bunch of sturdy wood signs that simply said PLEASE-DON'T FEED THE ANIMALS.

They put them all over the park so that no matter where you went you saw them.

"I think this will help a lot," said Buck as he wiped the work sweat from his forehead.

"I fully agree," responded Ranger Leon. "And again I thank you for all your help and insight. Buck, you really know the woods, love the animals, and appreciate the natural way of life. And, I want to go fishing with you again, real soon."

"Anytime, Leon," said Buck as they shook hands. "It is starting to get late and I need to head back home before

the dark sets in. I carry a flashlight but it is always easier to walk through the woods with a little light out." They said goodbye to each other and Buck headed back down the trail that led from the city to the woods.

Rascal, who had been patiently waiting in a tree all day, spotted Buck coming down the trail, climbed down from the tree and ran to meet him. "How did it go, Buck? What happened? You look tired like you have been working all day."

"Yes, I am tired," responded Buck. "I will tell you all about it on our way home." And he did. All the way back Buck told Rascal about what he saw in the park, meeting his old friend Ranger

Leon, and how they built and put out signs all day. Rascal just walked along, listened, and was glad that he had been involved.

"Rascal, if it wasn't for your good detective work we would have

Good job Rascal!

Thanks Buck.

never found out what the problem was. Thanks again," said Buck as he gave Rascal a little pat on his head.

"Tomorrow you should go out and find your friends Ollie Opossum, Jackie Pheasant, and Clyde Swan and let them know what happened. They will be happy to find out why they got pelted on their heads with nuts and what happened with the squirrels. Oh yeah, you should also stop by and visit old Grandpa Grady Gray Squirrel and explain to him. He should be very happy when the squirrels return to the woods and start being normal again. They have a lot of nuts to clean up—the natural way!"

CHAPTER 10

BACK TO THE NORMAL WAY

That night Buck and Rascal got back to the tree house safe and sound and had a good sleep. Rascal dreamt about climbing the biggest tree in the forest and Buck dreamt about catching the biggest fish ever. It took a little time, about a week or so, and things started to slowly come back to normal. The signs in the park had done their job, people became more aware and the feeding of wild animals had come to a stop. Slowly and very reluctantly all of the animals

returned to their natural way of finding food, including the squirrels. The squirrels missed all of the free cashews, peanuts, and macadamia nuts, but as they started to get hungry again they quickly went back to their natural way of food gathering. They even felt better about themselves and much healthier. Slowly but surely they all returned back to the woods, went back to their old home and their natural way of life. Old Grandpa Grady Gray Squirrel once again had a big smile on his face knowing that all the animals were back in their proper place.

Everything went back to normal. Life again in the woods was smooth and easy. Animals came to visit Buck, Buck went fishing, and Rascal took long naps. Everything was just fine for a long time until one day Lucy and Sadie, the twin sister robins, came to visit Buck with a problem they were having in the woods. It seems they couldn't find their favorite natural food to eat, the worms. They were gone—just vanished! The rumor in the woods was that the worms went fishing and didn't come back.

Join Buck Wilder in his next outdoor adventure story while he helps to solve the problem as to why 'The Worms Went Fishing.' Until then, keep a smile on your face, and make everyday count!

Throw the frowns away!

SECRET MESSAGE DECODING PAGE

Hidden in this book is a secret Buck Wilder message. You need to figure it out. Hidden in many of the drawings are letters that, when put together, make up a statement, a Buck Wilder statement. Your job is to find those letters and always remember the message—it's important.

DO NOT write in this book if it's from the library, your classroom, or borrowed from someone.

If you need help finding the hidden letters turn the page.

☐☐☐   ☐☐☐
☐☐☐☐☐☐   ☐☐☐

16 letters make up 4 words.

The secret letters are hidden on the following pages in this order…

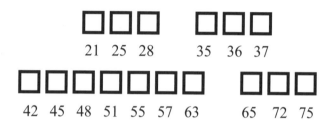

21 25 28   35 36 37

42 45 48 51 55 57 63   65 72 75

16 letters make up 4 words.

Remember—Don't Write in this Book!